Dear Parent:

Congratulations! Your child is taking the first steps on an exciting journey. The destination? Independent reading!

STEP INTO READING® will help your child get there. The program offers five steps to reading success. Each step includes fun stories and colorful art. There are also Step into Reading Sticker Books, Step into Reading Math Readers, Step into Reading Phonics Readers, Step into Reading Write-In Readers, and Step into Reading Phonics Boxed Sets—a complete literacy program with something for every child.

Learning to Read, Step by Step!

Ready to Read **Preschool–Kindergarten**
• big type and easy words • rhyme and rhythm • picture clues
For children who know the alphabet and are eager to begin reading.

Reading with Help **Preschool–Grade 1**
• basic vocabulary • short sentences • simple stories
For children who recognize familiar words and sound out new words with help.

Reading on Your Own **Grades 1–3**
• engaging characters • easy-to-follow plots • popular topics
For children who are ready to read on their own.

Reading Paragraphs **Grades 2–3**
• challenging vocabulary • short paragraphs • exciting stories
For newly independent readers who read simple sentences with confidence.

Ready for Chapters **Grades 2–4**
• chapters • longer paragraphs • full-color art
For children who want to take the plunge into chapter books but still like colorful pictures.

STEP INTO READING® is designed to give every child a successful reading experience. The grade levels are only guides. Children can progress through the steps at their own speed, developing confidence in their reading, no matter what their grade.

Remember, a lifetime love of reading starts with a single step!

5 Classic Golden Book Tales

Published in the United States by Random House Children's Books, a division of Penguin Random House LLC, 1745 Broadway, New York, NY 10019, and in Canada by Penguin Random House Canada Limited, Toronto.

The works in this collection were originally published separately by Random House Books for Young Readers as follows: *The Poky Little Puppy* in 2015, *The Shy Little Kitten* in 2015, *Tawny Scrawny Lion* in 2016, *Scuffy the Tugboat* in 2017, and *Tootle* in 2017. The Poky Little Puppy, The Shy Little Kitten, Tawny Scrawny Lion, Scuffy the Tugboat, and Tootle are trademarks of Penguin Random House LLC.

Step into Reading, Random House, and the Random House colophon are registered trademarks of Penguin Random House LLC.

Visit us on the Web!
StepIntoReading.com
rhcbooks.com

Educators and librarians, for a variety of teaching tools, visit us at RHTeachersLibrarians.com

ISBN 978-0-525-64516-0

MANUFACTURED IN CHINA

10 9 8 7 6 5 4

Random House Children's Books supports the First Amendment and celebrates the right to read.

5 Early Readers!

STEP INTO READING®

5 Classic Golden Book Tales

Step 1 Books
A Collection of Five
Early Readers

Random House New York

Contents

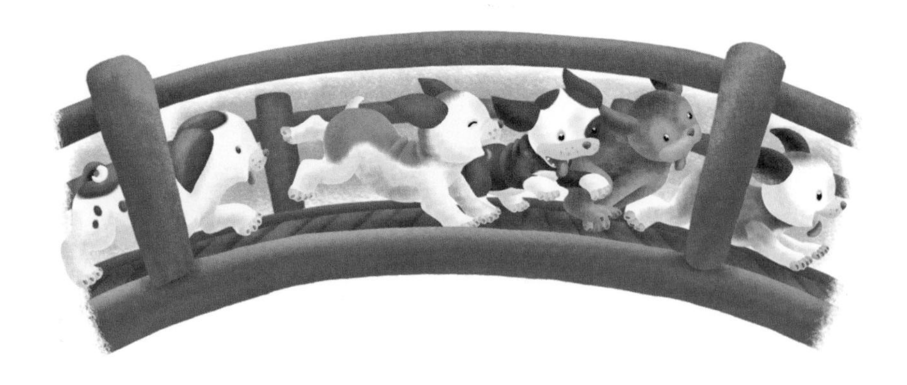

STEP INTO READING®

STEP 1 READY TO READ

The POKY LITTLE PUPPY

adapted by Kristen L. Depken
illustrated by Sue DiCicco

Five little puppies.

Dig, dig, dig!

Under the fence.

Into the meadow.

Run, run, run!

Down the road.

Over the bridge.

Across the green grass.

Up the hill.

Two by two.

One, two,

three, four puppies.

Where is that
poky little puppy?

Is he
on this side?

No.

A little snake!

Is he
on that side?

No.

A big grasshopper!

There he is!

Run, run, run!

Roly-poly.

Pell-mell.

Tumble-bumble.

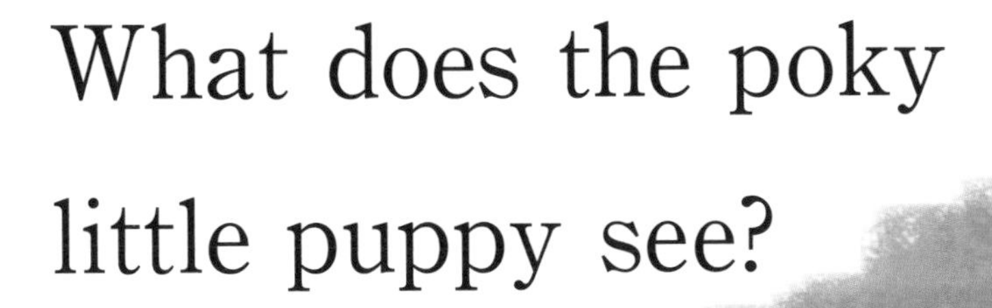
What does the poky
little puppy see?

A big red strawberry!

The puppies are hungry!

Run, run, run!

Across the green grass.

Over the bridge.

Up the road.

Into the meadow.

Under the fence.

Fill up the hole!

Home, sweet home!

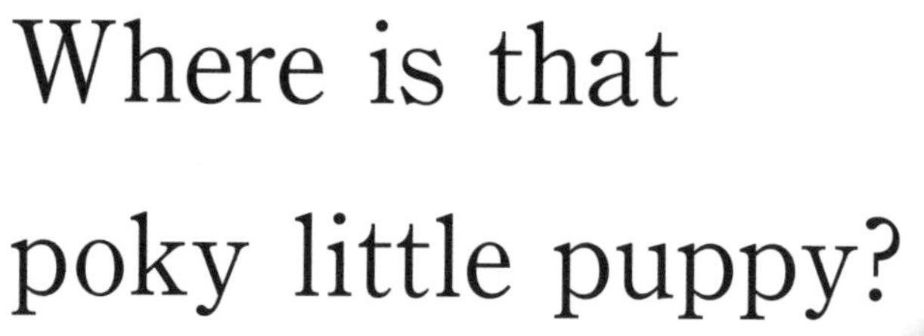

Where is that
poky little puppy?

STEP 1 READY TO READ

STEP INTO READING®

The Shy Little Kitten

adapted by Kristen L. Depken
illustrated by Sue DiCicco

One mama cat.

Six little kittens.

Black-and-white.

One has stripes.

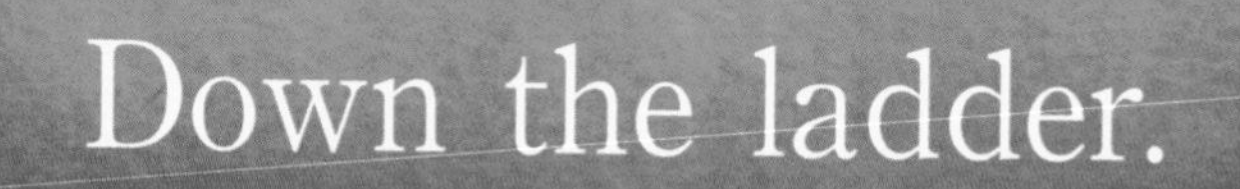
Down the ladder.

Jump, jump, jump!

Onto the grass.

Roll, roll, roll!

The little striped kitten
is very shy.

Pop!

A chubby mole!

They go
for a walk.

Green frog.

Big mouth!

The mole and the kitten laugh and laugh.

Bounce, bounce!

A shaggy puppy!

Where is the mama cat?

The shaggy puppy knows!

"Woof, woof!"

A red squirrel!

“Chee, chee, chee!”

Down the hill.

Hop, hop, hop!
Across the brook.

Onto the farm.

Mama cat!
One, two, three, four,
five, six little kittens.

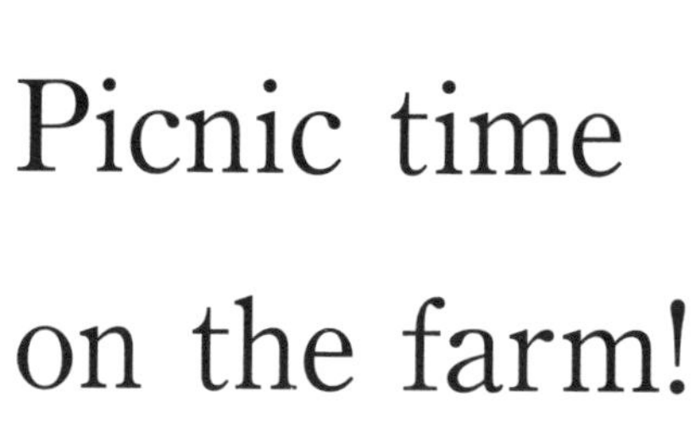

Picnic time
on the farm!

Seeds for the chickens and ducks.

Carrots for the rabbits.

Mash for the pigs.

Berries and milk for the little kittens!

Uh-oh.

PLOP!

PLOP!

SPLASH!

All the animals
laugh and laugh.

Best day ever!

STEP INTO READING®

STEP 1 READY TO READ

TAWNY SCRAWNY LION

adapted by Kristen L. Depken
illustrated by Sue DiCicco

The tawny, scrawny lion
is always hungry.

Run, run, run!

He chases monkeys

on Monday.

Kangaroos on Tuesday.

He chases zebras
on Wednesday.

Bears on Thursday.

Elephants on Saturday.

Run, run, run!

The lion is still hungry!

“Stop chasing us!”
say the animals.

“Stop running,”
says the lion.

Hop, hop, hop.
A brave little rabbit
talks to the lion.
"You look scrawny,"
he says.

So he asks the lion
to eat supper
with his family.
Carrot stew!

Carrot stew?

Yuck!

Rabbits?

Yum!

The lion says yes.

The lion follows
the rabbit.

Herbs and berries!
The rabbit picks some
for dinner.

Then he stops
to catch fish
for the stew.

At last
they reach
the rabbit's house.

The lion is so hungry!

The lion sees something
he would like to eat!
More rabbits!

Hop, hop, hop!

The rabbits bring the lion

some carrot stew.

It smells good.
It tastes good.
The lion eats bowl
after bowl!

Time for berries!
The lion eats
lots of berries,
too.

The tawny, scrawny lion
is not scrawny anymore!

The lion walks home.
He is good and fat
and full.

He will not eat
animals anymore.

The animals are
so happy!
They thank
the little rabbit.

But what will
the tawny lion
eat now?

More carrot stew!

STEP
1
READY TO READ
STEP INTO READING®
Scuffy
THE TUGBOAT
adapted by Kristen L. Depken
illustrated by Sue DiCicco

Scuffy is
a little red tugboat.
He does not want
to live in a toy store.
He wants
something bigger!

Scuffy meets a man
with a polka-dot tie.

He takes Scuffy home to his little boy.

“Sail, little tugboat,”
says the boy.
But Scuffy will not sail
in a bathtub.

A brook!

Now Scuffy will sail.

Scuffy sails away fast.
"This is the life for me!"
he toots.

Scuffy sails
past flowers.

He sails

past woods.

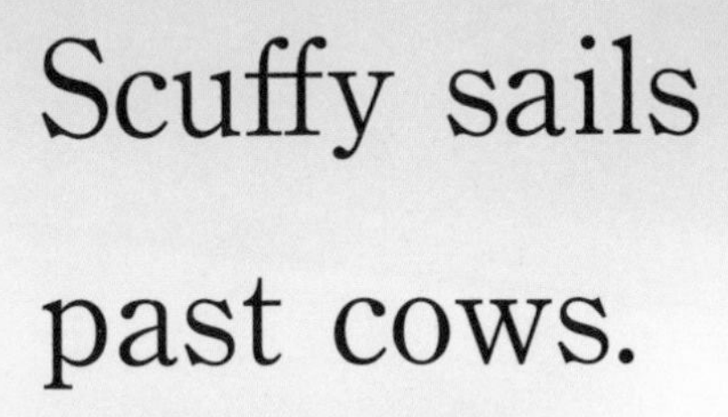

Scuffy sails
past cows.

A cow tries
to drink Scuffy!
That is not fun.

Hoot, hoot!

An owl!

Scuffy is scared.

The brook turns
into a river.

Now Scuffy sails
past a small town.

Scuffy sails past logs. Ouch!

The river gets bigger and busier.

Scuffy sails
under tall bridges
and past a big town.

He is proud
of his wide river!

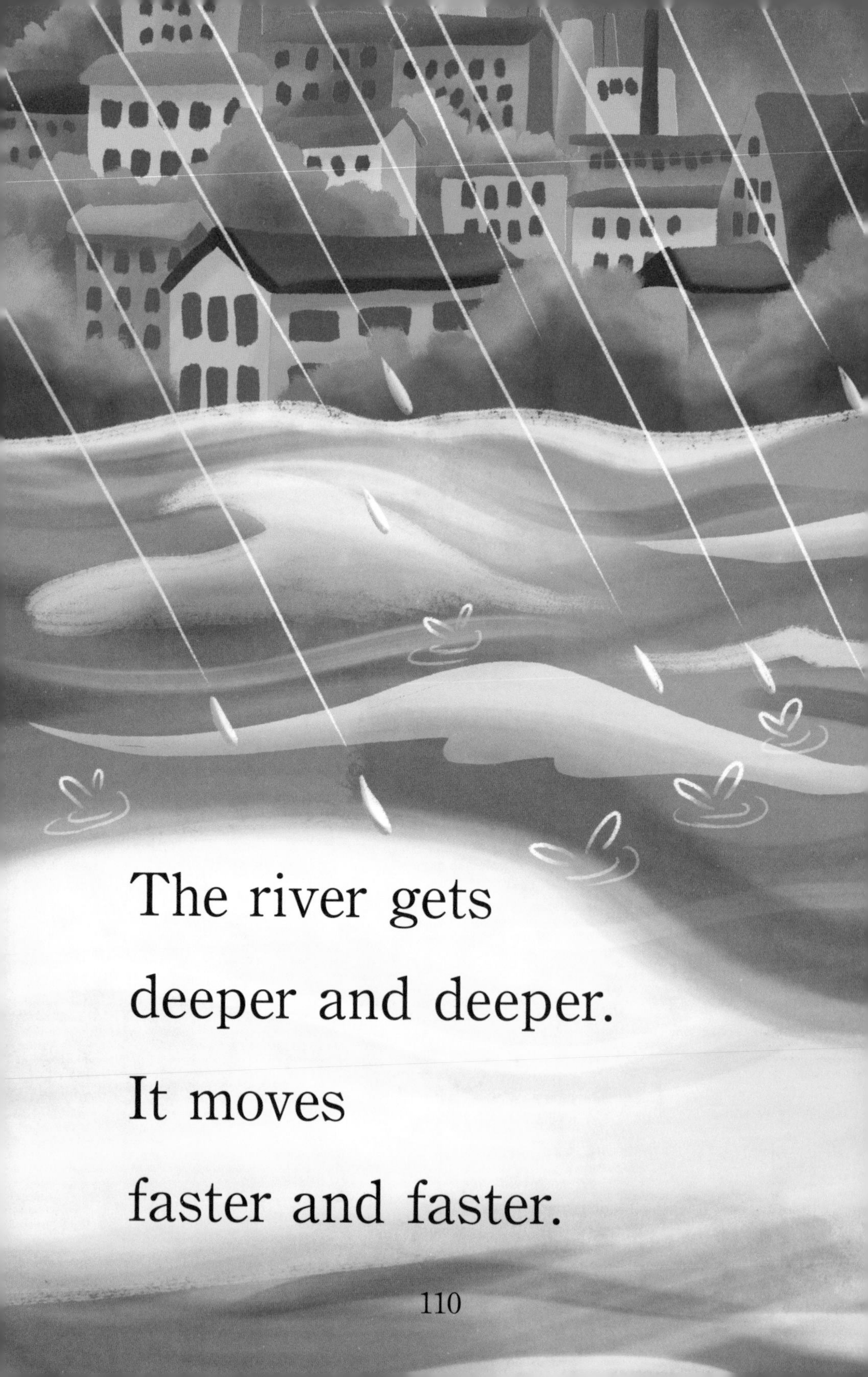

The river gets
deeper and deeper.
It moves
faster and faster.

Scuffy moves faster,

too.

A flood!
The river grows
higher and higher.
The people try
to stop it.

Now Scuffy sails
into a big city.

It is busy and noisy!

Toot, toot!

No one hears Scuffy.

He misses the man

with the polka-dot tie.

He misses the boy.

“Oh, oh! The sea!”
cries Scuffy.

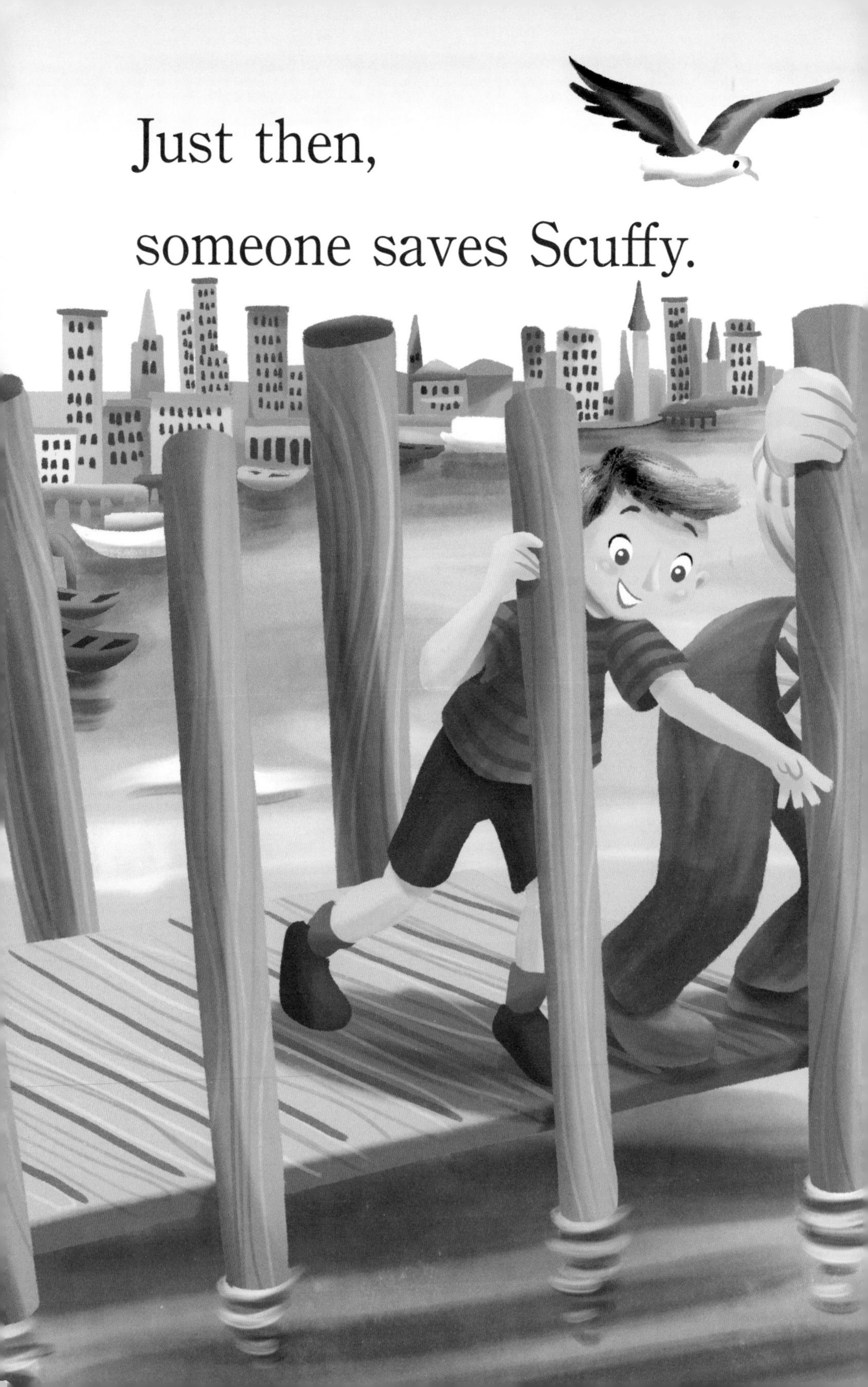

Just then,

someone saves Scuffy.

It is the man
with the polka-dot tie!
He takes Scuffy home.

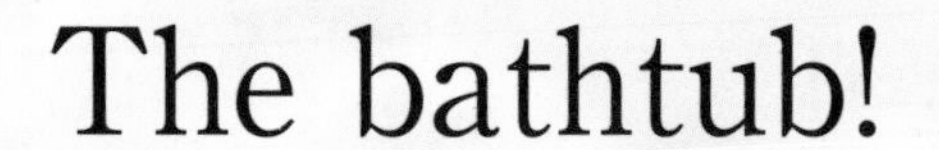

The bathtub!

“This is the life for me!”

Scuffy toots.

STEP 1 READY TO READ

STEP INTO READING®

TOOTLE

TOOTLE

adapted by Tennant Redbank
illustrated by Sue DiCicco

Train school!

Old Bill teaches

trains to . . .

SLOW
STOP
GO
STOP

Come around curves.

Stop for red flags.

Most of all?

Stay on the rails,

no matter what!

Good trains work hard
to stay on the rails.

Tootle works hard.

He loves to go fast!

But stopping for
red flags?
No fun!

“Race you!”
a horse shouts.

TOOTLE

The horse runs straight.

The rails curve.

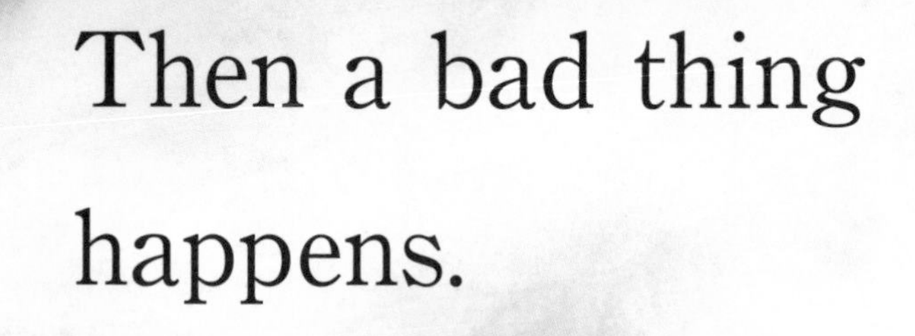

Then a bad thing happens.

Tootle hops
off the rails!

The meadow is nice.
It is full of
buttercups.
Tootle goes
into the meadow
again and again.

He chases butterflies.

He picks flowers.

Stay on the rails, Tootle!

The Mayor himself

has seen you.

Bill has a plan
to keep Tootle on track.
Everyone helps.

Tootle leaves the rails.

He sees a red flag.

STOP!

He turns.

STOP!

Another red flag!

He turns again.

STOP!

Red flags are everywhere!

No fun!

Look!

A green flag.

It is on the rails.

TOWN HALL
STOP
LOOK
AND
LISTEN

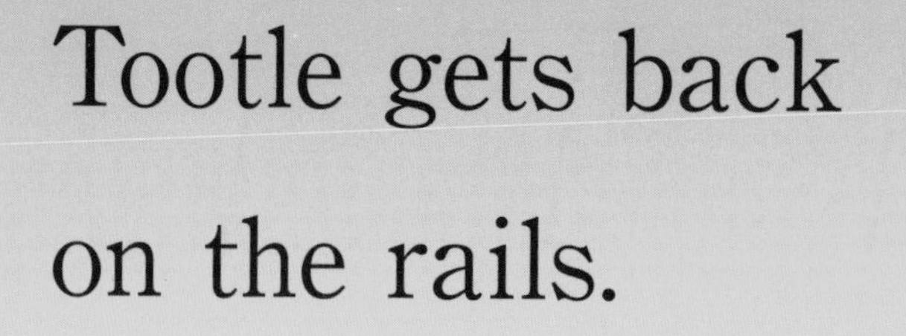

Tootle gets back

on the rails.

"This is the place for me,"

Tootle tells Bill.

Now Tootle stays
on the rails,
no matter what.

Hooray for Tootle!